THE
DEAD ATE
CHEESE

The Dead Ate Cheese

https://thedefpix.com/

Book Cover by Def Pix Entertainment

Editing: EJL Editing

Beta Reader: Paola Llerenas

Print edition ISBN: 979-8-9889373-0-2

E-book edition ISBN: 979-8-218-25579-4

WARNING; This book features graphic depictions of zombie related violence. You have been warned.

Dedicated to AF & MTW

Love you

THE
DEAD ATE
CHEESE

ERIC WILLIFORD

Def Pix Entertainment

Table of Contents

Prologue

It's the time of year when everyone at Dairy International tries to make up for fifty weeks of cat videos and porn. The sterile and drab conference room sits on the top floor. White on white on white. An overpriced monstrosity of a conference table sits in the middle of the room.

In the middle of the table, a young executive feigns confidence as he shuffles through papers. Everyone around the table watches him. Bored to tears. He clears his throat. Glances around the table. "It's called Soychup," the young executive says. "Sixty percent ketchup, forty percent soy sauce. A hundred percent delicious. We put the ketchup and the soy sauce into the same bottle. Shake it up. Slap a label on it, and boom! We have a condiment that's perfect for everything from French fries to Kung Pao Chicken. I've got some mockups I can pass around."

The young executive flips through his folders.

Seated at the head of the table, the CEO sighs. Hair pulled into a tight bun. Her seven-hundred-dollar Scanlan Theodore black short sleeve polo dress is tailored to perfection. "That won't be necessary. Does anybody have anything less... idiotic?"

Silence and blank stares.

The CEO leans forward and eyes those gathered around the table. "I've got the shareholders' meeting in a week. There will be massive layoffs if I don't take them something new and exciting. Including many of the people who work under you."

Everyone at the table averts their eyes. Desperate to avoid her gaze.

"And if there are fewer people," she says, "they'll take out the vending machines."

The vending machine threat sends a charge through the room. A bookish man dressed in a lab coat raises his hand. "I may have something."

The CEO shifts in her seat and prepares herself for whatever nonsense gets hurled her way. "Is it better than pouring soy sauce into a ketchup bottle?"

The scientist keeps his focus on the charts and graphs laid out in front of him. "I believe so," he says. "I've been working on a side project with a colleague from R&D. We may have discovered a way to extend the shelf life of cheese by as much as forty percent."

The CEO sits back. "What type of cheese?"

"All of it."

Chapter One

6 Months Later

The gas station sits on the side of the highway. Run by the same family for generations. Untouched by the grubby little paws of corporate America.

A trio of crows cut their way through the gray skies.

At one of the three pumps stands Gabby. She fills the tank of her five-year-old Honda Civic. She's dressed like a badass contestant on a cooking competition show. Complete with ripped jeans and a plain white t-shirt under her leather jacket. Crafting scissors chopped her blonde hair an inch below the jawline.

Something in the back seat of the car has her attention. Whatever it is, she stares at it. Lost in thought.

Click.

The pump cuts off. Gabby checks the gauge—a hair under thirteen gallons. Full tank. She returns the pump to its rightful home. Freezes at the sight of something in the distance.

A construction worker shuffles across the Dollar Store parking lot. He pukes his guts out but is unfazed. His bright orange vest now covered in bright green sick.

"My guess, heroin."

Gabby turns to the source of the voice. She watches as Nadia arrives next to her with arms full of snacks. Chips. Fountain drink. Cookies. Her wavy black and brown hair hangs below her shoulders. She's dressed in a perfectly faded vintage turntable t-shirt with red yoga pants. Brightly colored nightclub wristbands cover her arms. A sharp contrast against her brown skin. She extends the fountain drink. "Taste it."

Gabby accepts the drink and sips from the straw. "Sprite with a—"

"Dash of orange soda," Nadia smirks. "I know what my girl wants."

"I don't deserve you."

Nadia motions to the car. "Wanna make out on the hood?"

Gabby points to the construction worker across the street. "What about him?"

"We can charge him to watch. Earn some gas money."

Gabby stares at the construction worker. "I'm not trying to get thrown up on."

"Way to kill a mood, Gabby."

Gabby clocks the array of snacks. "If you're hungry, we can get real food."

"This is real food."

Gabby makes her way to the driver's side door. The item in the backseat becomes visible. A bouquet. "I could go for a burger."

The assortment of snacks makes it hard for Nadia to open the passenger side door. "We got time for that?"

"My folks ain't going nowhere."

#

An authentic diner. Sticky floors and various aromas fill the air. Fried finger foods. Grease. Day-old coffee.

At a booth in the back corner, a bored server holds a pen in one hand and a notepad in the other as she stares straight ahead.

Gabby takes a sip from her water. "Where did you hear that?"

"Moose."

Gabby scoffs. "The bartender?"

"He's a bouncer."

The server glances at her neglected tables. "I can come back."

Nadia motions at Gabby. "She'll have a hamburger."

The server jots down the order.

Gabby says, "Cheeseburger."

The server crosses out 'hamburger' and replaces it with 'cheeseburger.'

"I'm not gonna change my diet," Gabby says, "because of something you read on a fringe website."

"Just do me this one favor, okay?"

The women glare at each other. Each waits for the other to flinch.

"I got other tables."

Defeated, Gabby turns to the server. "Hamburger it is."

The server crosses out 'cheeseburger.' Reinstates hamburger as the meal of choice. She rushes to her next table before there's another change.

"When you're in New York,' Nadia says, "you and your chef friends can risk your lives with all the cheeseburgers you want."

"Thanks."

Nadia scans the rest of the diner. "I'm sure the cheeseburgers are better in the Big Apple, anyway."

"You sure this is what you want to do? Right now?"

Nadia turns back to Gabby. Shrugs.

Gabby seethes. "There's a whole world out there. I'm not gonna let you keep me from seeing it."

"Now I'm keeping you from... are you breaking up with me?"

Gabby scans the diner. There's a family seated five tables over. Mom. Dad. Two kids. The son is roughly eight years old. The daughter, two years younger. A chicken fried steak sits in front of the dad. The mom picks at her biscuits and gravy. The son downs a slab of French toast drenched in syrup, then steals a chicken tender off his sister's plate. She pleads with her parents to make him give it back.

"Are you?"

Nadia's demand brings Gabby's attention back to her own table. "That's not... I didn't want..." She collects herself. "I didn't mean to be hurtful."

"I thought we were going to try the long-distance thing?"

Gabby shifts in her chair. Eyes dart across the diner once again. "Forget I said anything."

"You bring me out to the middle of nowhere to break up with me before you move? You're a class act, Gabby."

Gabby grabs her silverware. Flips the butter knife through her fingers. "This was supposed to be a fun road trip for the both of us."

Nadia stiffens. "A last hurrah before you flush five years down the toilet?"

The knife falls out of Gabby's hand. Clangs against the table. She grabs it and sets it to the side. Picks up her water. "Before I move to New York." She takes a sip from the straw.

Nadia exhales. Tears form in the corners of her eyes. She blots them with the tip of her finger. Gabby can see what's about to happen.

"The whole purpose of this," Gabby says, "is to convince you to come with me."

"I don't want to talk about it."

#

Nadia marches out of the diner and heads straight to the car. Gabby is close behind her—keys in hand.

As Gabby sticks the key into the door, she sees the construction worker with the vomit-covered vest shuffling towards an older lady. He twitches every few steps. The moment he's close enough, he lunges for her. The older lady screams. She pushes on the construction worker. Desperate to keep his teeth off her face. Gabby races to her aid.

Nadia cries out, "Gabby!" as she takes off after her.

Gabby arrives at the scuffle and grabs the construction worker from behind. With all her strength, she pulls him off the older lady. He groans and pushes Gabby off, then turns around to face her, ready to pounce.

The older lady hits him in the back of the head with her purse. Repeatedly.

Gabby takes a step back. "Cut it out, man."

The construction worker responds with a twitch as he takes another step toward her. The older lady hits him again with her purse. He turns to her and hisses. The old lady freezes.

Gabby flails her arms. "Focus on me, man."

He turns back to Gabby and tackles her to the ground. She hits the ground with him on top of her. She brings her forearm up to his neck to hold him at bay.

Nadia grabs a trash can from the front of the diner. Trash spills out of it as she lifts it up and flips it over.

With all the strength she can muster, Gabby pushes the construction worker off her. He stands and prepares to lunge at her again. She scrambles to her feet. Scans the area for a weapon.

Nadia races up from behind the construction worker and brings the trash can down over his head. It pins his arms to his sides. He hisses as he waddles back and forth.

Gabby turns to the older lady. "You got a car?"

The older lady replies with a nod. Affirmative. The trio wastes no time. Seconds later, they arrive at her car. The older lady pulls out her phone. Snaps a quick picture of Nadia and Gabby. "My son needs to see that there's still some good in this world. Thank you, darlings."

She gets into her car. Closes the door. Keys the ignition, and drives off.

The construction worker continues to waddle around until he bumps into another car and falls.

Gabby grabs Nadia's hand. "We need to get going."

They sprint to their car.

Chapter Two

Lust for Life spews out of the speakers.

Gabby grips the steering wheel with her right hand, and her left hand taps to the beat. The saltiness from the pickles and French fries coats her tongue as she uses it to rub the roof of her mouth.

Nadia gazes out the window as they make their way down the two-lane highway. A Ford Explorer sits on the side of the road. A newer model. Green with Pirelli tires. All the doors are open. Not a single person in sight.

Gabby can feel Nadia's eyes as they drill into the side of her head. She refuses to turn and face her. She grips the steering wheel. Knuckles whiten.

A murder of crows fills the sky. On the hunt for prey. Or a carcass to pick apart.

Nadia reaches over and turns down the radio. Iggy Pop fades into the background.

Gabby bobs her head to the music as she reaches over and turns the music back up.

#

Gabby grips the bouquet as she and Nadia trudge through the cemetery. The ground remains soggy from the previous day's downpour. Headstones pay homage to a wide variety of local legends. Civil War heroes and villains. Juvenile hackers. Tom who peaked in middle school. Helen with the three and a half cats. The 1997 Quilting Champion.

"Are we not going to talk about it?" says Nadia.

"Thought you didn't want to talk about it."

"Not that. The guy."

"Oh."

"There have been reports," Nadia says, "out of France. People vomiting and acting strange after they've eaten cheese. Acting similar to that guy outside of the diner."

"You want a trophy for making me order a hamburger? Applaud you for saving my life."

"Or you could just say thank you."

Gabby stops. Eyes a pair of gravestones up ahead. "Thank you."

"Take all the time you need."

Gabby exhales. Turns and makes her way to a pair of headstones. Nearby, the epitaph on another headstone reads:

Finally Some Sleep

Charles Browner 1908–1977

Gabby kneels down and divides the bouquet between the two graves.

Nadia wipes away a tear. Something catches her attention. A bride in a bloody wedding dress shuffles toward them. Twitches. On the other side of the cemetery, two bridesmaids shuffle towards them. Both covered in blood and green vomit. Both hiss. Both twitch.

Gabby doesn't realize there is a groom headed straight for her. Green vomit covers his gray sports coat.

Nadia scans the area. Her eyes dart from the bride to the bridesmaids to the groom. Panic sets in. "We need to wrap this up."

Gabby stands. Finally notices the groom. "Something I can help you with?"

"He doesn't want help. We need to get to the car," says Nadia.

Gabby takes the hint. Rushes over to Nadia, and the pair head to the car. They evade the bride and her bridesmaids as they sprint across the cemetery. The car never comes into view. Instead, they see an entire wedding party. Fancy clothes covered in blood and green vomit. All of them twitch. All of them shuffle. All of them stand between Nadia, Gabby, and the car.

Gabby stops in her tracks. Grabs Nadia's arm. "This way."

She drags Nadia into the nearby woods.

#

The woods are thick with trees, roots, and foliage. Nadia and Gabby enter in a full sprint. There's no path. They dodge branches as they head deeper into nature.

"We should double back," Nadia says. "Come up on the opposite side of those things and hop in the car."

"What if they're still surrounding the car?"

Nadia picks up a stick. "We can fight them off."

Gabby grabs a rock the size of a mango. There's a noise in the distance. They wait in silence. Mango-sized rock and stick at the ready.

No sign of movement.

Nadia whispers. "We need to head that way." She points to the right. They head in that direction. Two dozen steps later, Gabby grabs her arm.

"Listen." Gabby places a finger to her lips.

Feet drag along the ground. Accompanied by hisses. The sounds draw nearer. Out of the brush, two fishermen shuffle towards them. They hiss and twitch as they approach. Blood and green vomit cover their waders. Nadia tightens her grip on the stick.

"Let's go around," says Gabby.

They hustle around the fishermen in a wide loop. The trees and brush blend as they run. In woods this thick, it's easy to get confused. Or lost. They slow to a walk.

Nadia says, "You realize what's going on, don't you?"

"Don't say it."

"Back there," Nadia says, "that thank you was ironic, wasn't it?"

"I know you're not happy."

"About being dumped or running for our lives?"

"Both." Gabby tries to get her bearings. "Neither. I don't know. What do you want me to tell you?"

"Tell me you're not going to take the job."

"You want me to pass on the biggest opportunity I've ever had to do what? Stay here and do nothing?"

Nadia stiffens. "That what this is? Nothing?"

Gabby tries to figure out which way is north. "This is me trying to figure out how to get back to the car."

"No. This is you trying to avoid the conversation."

"I don't know if you've heard,"—Gabby sighs—"but there's plenty of clubs for you to DJ at in New York."

"I prefer the clubs I play at now." Nadia studies Gabby. "You have no idea how to get back to the car, do you?"

"Do you?"

Nadia tests the weight of her stick. Gives it a swing.

"No surprise there." Gabby surveys the area. "If we head north, we should get back to the cemetery. Or, we can spend the rest of our lives waiting here."

"Funny."

Gabby smirks.

"For what it's worth," Nadia says, "there's nobody I'd rather be lost with."

"Now you're just buttering—"

"Help!" A man's voice pleads in the distance. "Is there someone there? Please. Help."

Gabby and Nadia argue in silence. Each states their case with wild gestures and exaggerated facial expressions. Gabby wants to help. Nadia does not.

"Please. I can hear you."

Gabby heads towards the voice. Nadia follows her. Stick ready for battle.

Chapter Three

The jogger sits with his back to the tree. Yellow headband above his brow. Compression leggings under his shorts. Overpriced Nike's on his feet. A chunk of his calf is gone. In its place, exposed muscles and fat. Blood drips on the ground. He grimaces from the pain. "I thought he needed help. Before I knew it, guy bit a chunk out of my leg."

Gabby struggles as she helps him to his feet. "Nadia!"

Nadia arrives next to them and helps Gabby hoist him to his feet. She's careful not to get blood on herself.

"Thank you," says the jogger.

Gabby remains next to him. A shoulder to lean on. "The guy who bit you. Where is he now?"

"Not sure. I was able to get away. Adrenaline before the pain set in."

Nadia checks herself for the man's blood. "Was the guy who bit you the only person you've seen acting this way?"

"You saying there's more than one person acting this way?"

"Afraid so," says Gabby.

The trio makes their way through the dense forest. The jogger relies on Gabby and Nadia for every step he takes. Their pace is deliberate. In the distance is a deer. On its side. Dead. A man and woman are on their knees next to the deer. Both are dressed for a hike. The man pulls out a handful of deer entrails. Crams them into his mouth. The woman tears at the deer's flesh with her teeth. Fur sticks to the deer blood on their faces.

"My god," says the jogger.

Gabby pulls them to the left. "We'll go around."

After only a few steps, the jogger heaves. Gabby tries to keep him upright. "Keep it together, man."

He heaves again. Green vomit gushes out of his mouth. A geyser that splatters onto the ground. Nadia leaps out of the way, and the jogger loses his balance. As he falls, he pulls Gabby down with him. Her rock falls to the side. She tries to get up as the jogger hisses. He pulls himself on top of her. She uses both her hands to hold back his face. He tries to lick her face. His tongue is only inches from her eye.

A stick hits the side of the jogger's face. It snaps in two. Nadia discards the broken piece that remains in her hand. The jogger turns and hisses at her for a moment but turns back to Gabby. Residual green vomit spills out of his mouth and onto Gabby.

Nadia grabs the mango-sized rock.

Desperate to eat Gabby for lunch, the jogger never sees the rock that bashes him in the side of the head. He's thrown off Gabby. Lands on his back.

In an instant, Nadia is on top of him. Fury overtakes her. She howls as she brings the rock down on his face. Blood sprays her. The jogger tries to grab her. She brings the rock down on his face again.

And again.

And again.

More and more blood sprays her.

Nadia pulverizes the jogger's face.

Gabby watches in horror.

The rock continues to smash what's left of the jogger's face.

Gabby pulls Nadia off the corpse. "He's dead, Nadia. He's dead."

Nadia drops the rock. Shakes. "I... I couldn't stop."

"You saved my life."

"I lost control."

"You did what you had to—"

A hiss pierces the air. They turn to the jogger. It wasn't him. He has no face to hiss from.

Another hiss.

The hikers have left the deer and are headed right for them.

Gabby grabs Nadia. Drags her off into the woods, away from the new threat. As they make their way, the sounds of moans and hisses are all around them.

The edge of the woods is up ahead. A cabin comes into view.

#

Gabby attempts to open the front door to the cabin. It's locked.

Nadia bangs on the door. "Anybody in there?"

"Help! Open up!" Gabby tries the doorknob again. Still locked.

" I think I hear someone."

The door is flung open. On the other side, Allen towers over them. His distinct features passed down from generations of Nigerian ancestry. His white V-neck shirt is spotted with blood. He motions for them to enter. They do. He shuts the door behind them and locks it.

The scent of pork fat from the morning's breakfast pollutes the air. The cabin has seen better days. Circa 1993. One story. Open concept. The walls are covered with brown paint that will peel if you gaze at it long enough. A Sangean WR-11SE AM/FM tabletop radio sits on the mantel. A hallway leads to the bedroom and bathroom. Quaint. Perfect for shut-ins.

"Thank you," says Nadia.

"The two of you," Allen says, "have been through a lot, haven't you?"

On the couch sits a shell of a woman. Same complexion as Allen's and roughly the same age. It's the face of a woman who's been crying nonstop. Blood-stained hands grip a stuffed frog that's covered in blood. Gabby can't take her eyes off her. "It's been a day."

"I'm Allen." He points to the woman on the couch. "That's my wife, Carla."

Carla doesn't acknowledge the newcomers.

"I'm Nadia. This is my ex, Gabby."

Gabby bristles at the new label. "This your place?"

"Uh. No," says Allen. "We found it. Same as you."

"We the only ones here?" asks Gabby.

"Yeah. Got here about twenty minutes ago. Door was unlocked. We thought it was strange. But under the circumstances, figured we'd treat it as a blessing."

Gabby takes out her phone and dials a number and puts it to her ear, and lowers it again. "How is 911 busy?"

"I haven't been able to reach anyone all day," Allen says. "No friends. Family. Nothing."

Gabby turns to Nadia. "You got anything?"

"Left my phone in the car." She scans the room. "There a bathroom? I need to clean this nastiness off me."

"Down the hall." Allen points. "Can't miss it."

#

Nadia washes her hands in the sink and then pulls them out from under the water. She stares at them as they shake.

"Everything okay?" says Gabby from the doorway.

"What do you think?" She dries her hands with the towel.

"You had to kill him, Nadia."

"Wanna know why?" Nadia says. "Because you have a habit of making decisions without thinking about how they affect those around you." She tosses the towel aside.

Brushes past Gabby on her way out into the hallway, where she bumps into Allen. "Are you spying on us?"

"I wasn't spying. Or listening. Not on purpose. It's... it's my wife. Those things killed our daughter." He adjusts his shirt. "It hasn't even been two hours. That's why... that's why she's acting strange."

Nadia says, "For what it's worth, I'm sorry."

"I can't imagine," says Gabby.

"I just, I thought you should know."

Chapter Four

On an airstrip, two rows of soldiers stand at attention on either side of a red carpet. At the end of the carpet sits Air Force One. The Chief of Staff, an exhausted fifty-year-old man in a beige suit, stands at the foot of the stairs.

Next to him stands the Press Secretary, dressed in a crisp Anne Taylor black pants suit with a red blouse. She cradles a leather folder.

They watch as the door to the plane opens. Out steps the President of the United States. A man in his 60s dressed in a tailored suit that perfectly hugs his slender frame. Red tie. White shirt. Salt and pepper hair slicked back. He salutes and makes his way down the stairs.

Right behind him is Zora. His daughter. Blonde. Deep red lipstick. Early thirties. Gucci everything.

Behind them is the First Lady. Her top is a tad too low. Her skirt is a tad too high with a slit that's a tad too deep. Heels a tad too stripper-ish; jewelry a tad too gaudy. Age a tad too young. She stays two stairs behind the President and his daughter as she makes her way down.

The moment the President arrives on the carpet, the Chief of Staff and the Press Secretary flank him. "Mr. President. Zora," says the Chief of Staff.

The President doesn't stop. Eyes straight ahead. "What is it?"

"There have been some disturbing reports, sir." The Chief of Staff takes a sheet of paper from the Press Secretary. "From all over the country."

"It's nothing we can't handle, sir." The Press Secretary offers another sheet to Zora, who refuses it with a wave of her manicured hand.

The President salutes the soldiers as he goes. "Will this interrupt my fundraiser?"

"We are monitoring the situation," says the Chief of Staff.

Zora quickens her pace to catch up with her father. "What are the reports?"

"It appears," the Press Secretary says, "there have been cases of cannibalism breaking out all over the country."

Zora freezes. "Cannibalism?"

The Press Secretary draws even with her. "Some believe," she leans in close and whispers, "it's being caused by cheese."

The President keeps his eyes focused on what's in front of him. He salutes another soldier. "How is this affecting my polling?"

The Press Secretary says, "We haven't had time to conduct any polling, sir."

The President arrives next to a limo surrounded by Secret Service agents. "I'm sure it'll blow over. It's the media. I know it. They've been out to destroy me since I took office."

"Perhaps it would be best," Zora says, "if we don't mention cheese."

"Yes," the President says, "I don't want anyone mentioning the word cheese until this is over. Understood?"

The Chief of Staff glances at the Press Secretary and turns back to the President. "We'll see to it, sir."

Chapter Five

Gabby lies on the floor. Stretches her legs. "Did you see anything we can use to board this place up? Spare wood? Anything?"

Allen says, "I'm thinking we can take some doors down."

Nadia takes a seat next to Carla. "Does the frog have a name?"

"Mr. Giggles," Allen says. "We got him at a gas station about an hour before..."

Nadia turns to Carla—warmth in her eyes. "When I was a child, I used to put all my stuffed animals on the bed. They were my audience, and I'd sing for them. That's how I knew I wanted to do music."

Carla doesn't acknowledge her. Continues to stare straight ahead.

Allen turns on the radio. There's a moment of static, then the DJ speaks. His demeanor is calm. Eerie.

"...epidemic of mass murder being committed by an army of unidentified cannibals. The murders are taking place in villages, cities, rural homes, and the suburbs, with no apparent pattern or reason."

#

Nadia and Gabby search the kitchen cabinets and drawers. The DJ's voice fills the room.

"It seems to be a general explosion of mass homicide. There is speculation that the cannibalistic episodes are the direct result of eating cheese."

Nadia glances at Gabby. "Cheese. Imagine that."

Gabby replies with an epic eye roll. Turns her attention to a cardboard box. She kicks it over. Empty.

"Eyewitnesses say the cannibals are ordinary people. Some say they appear to be in some kind of trance."

Nadia finds a black marker inside a drawer. She sets it on the counter.

Gabby extracts a hammer from another drawer and holds it up for Nadia to see.

#

Allen sits next to Carla and places his arm around her shoulders. She doesn't acknowledge the gesture.

"Mayors in all major cities and the governors of more than twenty-five states have declared a state of emergency. Many of them have indicated that the National Guard may be mobilized. We are still awaiting a response from the federal government. Our only advice, please, for the love of god, stay in your homes. Lock the doors. Hug your loved ones—"

"Shut it off!" Carla says. "Please! Shut! It! Off!"

Allen jumps to his feet. Sprints to the radio and turns it off.

Gabby and Nadia race into the room.

"Everything okay in here?" Nadia says.

Carla catches her breath. Everyone waits for her to speak.

"The radio set her off," Allen interjects. "She's fine now."

"There's no food, and the only water," Gabby says, "is the tap. But I would advise against drinking it. There isn't much in the way of weapons, either. Found this." She holds up the hammer. "But that's about it."

Allen says, "According to the radio, this is happening all over the country."

"We heard," says Nadia, "guess we're on our own."

Gabby takes in the cabin. "Staying here isn't an option. We've got a car. It's back at the cemetery." She turns to Allen. "You know where that is?"

"Don't you?"

"We might have gotten a little lost," Gabby says.

"We can stay here." Nadia surveys the cabin. "See what happens. At least there's—"

Gunfire. From outside.

Gabby heads for the window. "Was that a gun?"

Allen is right behind her. "That was a rifle."

Another shot fires.

And another.

And another.

Chapter Six

Howell explodes out of the woods and heads straight for the cabin. A man in his fifties who cleans his gun more than himself. He's dressed in orange and green hunting gear. Hunting bag slung over his shoulder. Rifle in hand.

Hot on his heels is his son, Junior. Twenty-five and dressed in the same attire. No gun. Hunting bag slung over his shoulder. He overtakes his old man and reaches the door first. He tries the doorknob. It's locked. Bangs on the door. Frantic and desperate.

Howell turns to the woods. Raises his rifle. Waits.

A man in a dirty, green vomit-covered suit shuffles out of the woods. Howell unloads a round into his chest.

The door opens. Allen steps to the side as Junior plunges into the cabin.

Howell waits. Gun trained on the woods.

Dirty suit guy twitches. Howell shoots him again. This time in the head. Dirty suit guy twitches no more. Howell keeps his gun trained on the woods as he backpedals into the cabin. Once in, Allen shuts the door and locks it.

Gabby and Nadia take a moment to size up the new guests.

Howell lowers his weapon. "We appreciate ya'll lettin' us in." There is a tense moment as everyone but Carla sizes up each other. Junior sucks his teeth.

"I'm Howell. This is my son, Junior."

Junior waves.

"I'm Allen." He points to Carla. "My wife, Carla."

Junior steals a peek at Carla. "What's wrong with her?"

"We lost our daughter."

"Them things get yer girl?" Howell says.

Allen nods his head 'yes.'

"I'm Nadia. This is my—"

"Gabby."

Junior grins as he undresses them with his eyes. Nadia folds her arms over her chest.

Howell says, "Four of ya'll together?"

"Allen and Carla," Gabby says, "were here when we got here."

Howell shifts his gaze to Allen. "You broke into this cabin?"

"If we hadn't, you would have."

Howell moves his gaze from Allen to Nadia and Gabby. "Two of you together?"

"It's complicated," says Gabby.

Allen turns to Howell. "You're welcome to leave. Take your chances out there."

Howell surveys the cabin until his eyes land on his son. "We'll make do."

Nadia steps into the middle of the room. "Man on the radio says this is happening all over the country."

"Can't trust the media. Figure it's all some sort of hoax," says Howell.

Junior says, "The President will get it sorted."

Allen takes a seat next to Carla. "There hasn't been an official response from the federal government. Only the local—"

"I'm out of ammo, and the boy here lost his rifle. Might as well get comfortable. Wait for reinforcements." Howell selects a chair and has himself a sit.

Gabby laughs. "Reinforcements?"

Junior glares at her. "The President will get it sorted."

Nadia positions herself closer to Gabby. "We heard you the first time."

Gabby says, "There's no food. Or water. You all can stay here, but Nadia and I—"

"You speaking for me now?"

"I just thought..."

Nadia grabs Gabby by the arm. "Can I talk to you for a sec?" She drags Gabby into the furthest back corner of the kitchen. Wheels around to face her. "You don't speak for me."

"This isn't the—"

"Especially now that we're not even together."

Gabby sighs. "Oh. I see now. That's what this is about."

"Are you trying to make it about that?"

"Me? Okay then." Gabby straightens her back. "What, you're gonna stay here?"

"It's not a terrible idea."

"Eventually, those things will make their way to the house. And if they don't, you'll still starve to death. You willing to sit here and see which happens first?"

#

Howell watches Carla from his seat across the room. "That belong to yer kid?"

"Our daughter," says Allen.

Howell keeps his eyes on Carla. "How old?"

When Carla doesn't answer, Allen interjects. "Six."

Howell sits back in his chair. Stares at the stuffed animal in Carla's hand. "Cancer took my wife twelve years ago." He shifts his weight in the chair. Studies Junior for a moment. "That hole never fills. You just learn to stop putting stuff in it."

Junior takes out his hunting knife. Cleans it.

Gabby enters from the kitchen. Hammer in hand. "If we're gonna sit around in here, we should at least turn the radio on for updates."

Junior gets up. "I'll get it."

Nadia enters. Goes to the opposite end of the room, away from Gabby.

Howell notices the hammer in Gabby's hand. "You workin' on a craft project?"

"Sure am. I'm gonna build you a—"

"Gabby!" Nadia glares at her.

Howell grins at Gabby. She grins back.

The DJ's voice pours out of the radio. *"Because of the obvious threat to an untold number of citizens and because of the crisis that is currently developing, this radio station will remain on air day and night..."*

Howell pulls himself to his feet. "Ain't nothin' but lies. They just wanna control us, is all."

"... This station and hundreds of others will continue to pool our resources to keep you informed."

Chapter Seven

The First Lady stands by the mirror in the penthouse suite of an upscale resort. Her black, lacy thong is the only material on her body. She models for herself. Her assistant waits next to her. Clutches a red dress.

The First Lady waves her hand. A not-so-subtle sign that the red dress will not do. The assistant tosses the dress aside. Grabs a strapless red dress.

Another wave of the hand. Another dress discarded.

On the opposite side of the room, the President ties his tie. His suit appears to be the same as the one from earlier.

A knock at the door.

The President adjusts his tie. "What?"

The Chief of Staff and the Press Secretary enter. A Secret Service Agent closes the door behind them. The Press Secretary has her trusty leather folder.

The Chief of Staff notices the First Lady. Averts his eyes. "I'm so sorry. We can come back when the First Lady is dressed."

The President shoots a glance at his wife. "She's fine. What is it?"

The Press Secretary clears her throat. "The fundraiser... has been canceled."

"It's the cannibal situation, sir," says the Chief of Staff.

The President finally turns to face them. "You said it was under control."

"Not as much as we had hoped, sir." The Chief of Staff steals a peek at the First Lady as she dismisses another dress.

"What does this have to do with my fundraiser?"

The Press Secretary opens her folder. Reads from a sheet of paper. "Ninety-six percent of the invited guests have informed us they will not be attending."

The President is perplexed. "Because of the cannibals?"

The Press Secretary clears her throat again. "The remaining four percent are maybes. Their attendance depends on the menu. They want to know if we will serve items such as brie, mozzarella, feta, parmesan, foods of that nature."

The President makes no attempt to hide his growing fury. "I see what you did there. You're talking about cheese, aren't you?"

"You instructed us not to use that word, sir," says the Press Secretary.

"I'm the President. I can say it."

The First Lady finally selects a dress.

"There's panic, sir." The Chief of Staff struggles to keep his focus away from the First Lady. "In the cities. In the farmland. It's chaos."

"Perhaps," the Press Secretary says, "if you said something to calm the citizens. Ease their fears."

"If I said something, do you think we could get the donors to come back to the fundraiser?"

With the First Lady covered, the Chief of Staff gives his full attention to the President. "I don't see why not. Tell them the truth so they can protect themselves and their families."

"Tell them not to eat cheese? They'll accuse me of being a socialist. My base loves cheese. No. Find me someone to blame."

The Press Secretary whips out another piece of paper. "I've taken the liberty to compile a list of the top cheese-producing countries." She reads from the list, "Germany. The Netherlands. France. Italy. Denmark."

"Those won't work." The President paces. "Find me another country. Something less… European. What about a country in Africa? Or Asia?" He notices the First Lady. "You are a marvelous specimen."

She remains fixated on the mirror. Continues to model for her audience of one.

The President ogles her. "Round up the press. I know exactly what I'm going to say."

Chapter Eight

Chaos.

Everyone in the cabin talks over each other. The radio adds to the commotion. *"At this time, there is no way to say who or what to guard yourself against..."*

Howell is beside himself. "I don't understand why we're listening to this nonsense. It's all lies. Are you all too stupid—"

"Staying here is stupid." Gabby gestures to the door and windows. "But if that's what we're going to do, we need to fortify this place."

The DJ continues, *"... Law enforcement is overwhelmed and confused. We could not determine if any kind of organized investigation is underway..."*

"You can't trust any of them," Howell claims. "They're all part of a sex cult. A bunch of deviants."

Allen glances around the room. "Who are these deviants?"

Howell barks, "You know exactly who I'm talking about!"

"... Police, sheriff's deputies, and emergency ambulances are deadlocked with calls for help. The scenes around the country are that of total bedlam."

Allen searches for someone to make sense of Howell's claims. "Is he talking about politicians?"

Nadia stares at the radio. "I don't understand where things went so wrong."

Junior digs through his hunting bag. "The President will get it sorted. Watch."

Nadia whirls around to face Junior. "Stop saying that!"

"... Wait. I'm being told. Hold on. The federal government is preparing to issue a statement..."

Nobody in the room pays the radio any attention.

Gabby searches the room for something. "We need to put something over the windows so when they come, they can't see in."

Nadia pleads to anyone that will listen. "This wouldn't even be an issue if people would just stop eating cheese."

"... from the President, hold on. Yes. Okay. The President will hold a press conference..."

Howell can't take it. "This is America, damn it!"

"That has nothing to do with it," Allen says.

"... right now, we are standing by for a statement from the leader of the free world."

Gabby makes her way over to Nadia. "We need to take down all the doors from inside the house."

"And now, a word from the President of the United States."

Howell can't contain his excitement. "The President is about to say something. Everyone shut up. Show some respect!"

The room goes silent. Everyone turns to the radio.

Over the radio, the President speaks. His voice wavers. *"My fellow Americans. We find ourselves amid an unspeakable plague of cannibalism. Our towns, cities, and homes are under siege. But fear not, the numbers are not as bad as the media would have you believe..."*

Howell nods.

"... It may feel as though all hope is lost, but I want you to know that my administration, the greatest administration this country has ever seen, I might add..."

Allen takes a seat next to Carla.

"... They've done a great job. They truly have. And we are working with local and state officials to get this situation under control. According to the media, the cause of this is cheese. I have the best people, the smartest people, well-respected people, working on this..."

Junior swells with pride.

"... They have found no correlation between the eating of cheese and the current epidemic of cannibalism."

Gabby marches into the kitchen.

"... There is, however, compelling evidence that this is a strain of flu that was put here by Taiwan. I will see that we will respond appropriately. I will not let the Tai Flu destroy America. I have also created a Cannibalism Task Force, which will be led by my beautiful daughter,

Zora. Make no mistake; these are troubling times. This country will need your help to exterminate this cannibalistic threat. I need all of my freedom fighters to do what must be done. God bless America."

#

Gabby uses the claw on the hammer to pry the door off the cabinet under the sink.

Junior enters the kitchen. Hunting bag in hand. "Told you the President would get it sorted."

"Is that the only thing you're programmed to say?"

Junior undresses her with his eyes. "You and that other girl, Nicki—"

"Nadia."

"Right. You two are together, right?" He opens his bag. Rummages through it.

"Yeah."

"Like, together, together?"

"I guess."

He pulls a foil-wrapped sandwich out of the bag. "How'd you do it?"

"Do what?"

"Turn her. You know. Bring her over to the other side."

"Excuse me?"

"She don't seem like the recruitin' type."

"I whispered sweet nothings."

He grins and nods. "Respect." Then proceeds to unwrap the foil to reveal a ham and cheese sandwich.

Gabby watches as he takes a huge bite. "What are you doing?"

"I'm hungry."

"Please tell me there's no cheese in that."

"It's a ham and cheese."

Gabby grabs her hammer. Rushes out of the kitchen.

"What? The President said it was okay."

Gabby joins the rest of the group in the main room. "We got a problem. Dipshit is eating a ham and cheese sandwich."

Nadia gazes past Gabby and into the kitchen. "Where did he get a sandwich from?"

Howell picks up his hunting bag. "We brought them."

Junior joins them. "Can't hunt on an empty stomach."

Allen's protective instincts kick in. He jumps to his feet and steps in front of Carla. "Have you not been paying attention?"

"Have you?" Howell says. 'The President said it was safe to eat cheese. If my boy wants to eat a ham and cheese, that's his right as an American."

"Not if it puts us in danger.' Gabby fumes.

With a mouth full of sandwich, Junior says, "I don't see what the big deal is. Right, pops?'

"The government and the media," Howell says, "have no authority to tell us what we can and can't eat."

Nadia takes a step towards Gabby. "They can if it's killing people."

Junior takes another bite. With a mouth full of ham and cheese, he says, "You're all a bunch of socialists."

"They literally created the FDA for this reason," says Allen.

Junior makes a face.

Gabby sees that something is wrong with him. "He needs to quarantine until we can figure out what to do with him."

"We can lock him in the bathroom," Allen says.

"You're the one that broke into this cabin," Howell says. "We oughta lock you in the bathroom. Thug."

"What did you call me, old man?"

Junior has Nadia's full attention. "I think it's too late."

Everyone turns to Junior. He waves them off. "I'm fine. Little warm is all." He crams the last of his sandwich into his mouth and bends over as he swallows the last of it. He stands. Smiles. "It's just a sandwich."

"What have I been tellin' you all? Lies and deceit," says Howell.

Green vomit erupts out of Junior. Splatters onto the floor.

Allen pulls Carla back from the airborne liquid shrapnel. "Oh, shit!"

Junior doubles over. Clutches his stomach. Heaves. Vomits again. A torrent of green bile splashes onto the floor.

Howell makes his way over to him. "You alright, boy?"

"I'm fine." He vomits again. Crumbles to the floor.

Howell freezes. Reverses course.

"He's gonna turn," Nadia says. "We have to get him out of here."

Junior rises to his feet. Hisses. Sniffs the air.

"Junior?" Howell inches towards his bag.

His son responds with a hiss. Turns his attention to Carla. Hisses again.

"Go ahead," Carla says.

Junior prepares to lunge for her. But Allen grabs him from behind. Slides his forearm across his throat. Uses his other arm to hug Junior against his body.

Howell watches in horror. "You stop that right now, Junior!"

Gabby readies her hammer. "He's not Junior anymore." Takes two steps toward Junior and Allen.

Howell grabs her arm. "I'll do it." He takes the hammer from her.

Junior is desperate to snack on Carla. It takes all of Allen's strength to restrain him.

Howell says, "Turn him towards me and step back."

Allen spins Junior around to face Howell and pushes him forward, then steps back. Junior hisses. Twitches. Takes one shuffle step towards his dad.

Howell readies himself.

Junior hisses again. Closes the distance.

Almost there.

Howell waits for the perfect moment. He watches as Junior draws closer.

Junior hisses again. Before he can lunge, Howell brains him with the hammer and then pulls it out of Junior's skull.

Junior collapses to the floor. Dead.

Howell drops the hammer.

Allen takes a seat next to Carla. "You okay?"

Carla stares at Junior's body. "Why didn't you let him do it?"

"What?"

"We should have let him kill us. Then we could see her again."

Howell stares at Junior's body in disbelief. "It was the cheese. Ain't no damn Tai Flu. He lied to us. The President... lied to us."

"We need to bury him or burn him," says Allen.

"That's not my boy. Do whatever you want with that thing. But I ain't stickin' around to help." Howell gathers his things. "If he lied about the cheese, ain't no tellin' what else he's lyin' about. Ask me, ain't gonna be no reinforcements."

Gabby picks up her hammer. "Let's do this."

Howell pays her no attention as he slings his bag over his shoulder. "If we all go, we'll attract too much attention. I'll go. Come back with my truck. Then we all head out of here together."

"No offense," Allen says, "but how do we know you'll come back? Naw, man, I'm going with you."

Nadia says, "I'll go with him. Allen, you stay here with your wife."

Gabby grabs her arm. "I'm coming too."

"No. Just me and Howell. If you're here, Carla and Allen will know that I'm coming back."

"You using me as collateral?"

"Call it what you want." She tries to take the hammer out of Gabby's hand.

Gabby tightens her grip. "If you're trying to prove a point..."

"There's an entire world out there, remember?"

Gabby relinquishes her grip on the hammer.

Nadia turns to Howell. "Ready when you are."

Howell passes by Carla on his way to the door. She grabs his arm. Stands. Whispers something in his ear. When she's done, she returns to her seat on the couch.

Howell turns to Carla. "I appreciate the suggestion." He stoops down. Takes off Junior's watch. Puts it on.

Carla forces a smile.

Howell grabs his rifle.

Allen watches him. Suspicious. "Thought you were out of ammo?"

He flips it around. Holds it by the barrel. "I am."

Howell and Nadia venture out.

Chapter Nine

The final rays of sunlight ooze through the trees as the day gives way to dusk. Dozens of crows take flight and land in the trees above. Crows will hold a funeral for one of their own. Perhaps this is a celebration of life and not a harbinger of portent.

Nadia struggles to catch up to Howell as they make their way with weapons at the ready. "I'm sorry about your son."

"I appreciate it."

"He seemed to be a good guy."

"He was a little slow, but he had his moments."

Nadia finally catches up to him. "Before we left, what did Carla say to you?"

Howell keeps his eyes forward. Continues to trudge along. "Told me what I needed to hear." He eases into the silence that follows.

Nadia fidgets with the hammer. Uneasy with the silence. "You don't care for me very much, do you?"

"It's okay if everyone you meet doesn't take to you."

Nadia stops. "Can I ask you something?"

"Ain't that what you been doin'?"

"You're not thinking about killing me and then leaving with the truck, are you?"

Howell pauses but doesn't turn to face her. "Thought about it."

Nadia tightens her grip on the hammer. "And?"

Finally, he turns. Spits. "Asked myself, what would my son want?"

"The verdict?"

"He'd want me to make sure you got back to your girlfriend."

#

Gabby holds the feet, and Allen holds the shoulders as they carry Junior's body into the backyard.

"I'm not real excited about this," says Allen.

"If we don't bury him, he'll smell."

"Not this. How well do you know her?"

"Nadia?" Allen nods. She continues, "Is that what you're worried about? We've been together for five years. Trust me. She'll come back."

They lower the body onto the grass. Allen surveys the area. "Things seem tense between you two. She said you were her ex."

"It's been a long day. Besides, she's not gonna pass up a chance to rescue me and rub my face in it."

Allen uses his toe to measure the density of the ground. "This will have to do."

"Your wife gonna be okay?"

"Doubt it."

Inside the cabin, Carla remains on the couch. Junior's hunting knife sits on the floor. She leers at it for a moment. Then grabs it. Hides it under the couch cushions.

#

Dusk creeps in as Nadia and Howell proceed through the woods in silence. Crows and insects supply the soundtrack to their trek. Trees in the distance form ominous shapes. Shadows on the ground dance as squirrels jump from branch to branch.

Howell freezes. Holds up a hand. Nadia stops. He scans the area. Nadia listens. Readies her hammer.

A hiss. In the distance. Howell whispers as he motions to Nadia. "It's a ways off." He takes a step. Nadia grabs his arm. Signals for him to turn his head to the right. He does.

A businesswoman in a dirty white pants suit appears out of the brush. Speckles of green vomit dot the cuffs of her pants. She's headed right for them. Before Nadia can react, Howell springs into action. He brandishes his rifle akin to a baseball bat. Connects with the dirty businesswoman's head. Nadia flinches at the sound of her skull as it fractures.

The dirty businesswoman collapses to the ground. She only has time for one hiss before he pummels her head with the butt of his rifle.

Nadia watches as he gets the rage out.

After what feels like an eternity, he stops. Now covered in blood and exhausted, Howell exhales. "We should keep moving."

#

Allen paces the main room of the cabin. Wild hand gestures as he speaks. "All I'm saying is, we can't sit here and hope they come back."

"They'll be back. I know it," pleads Gabby.

Carla watches from the couch.

"Those things are gonna make their way to this cabin. We better not be here when they do," says Allen.

Carla says, "None of it matters."

Allen and Gabby turn to her. Shocked at her participation.

Carla's gaze bounces from Allen to Gabby. "All this arguing. It's a waste of time. A waste of energy. We're all gonna die."

"I'm not planning on dying," says Gabby.

Carla stares past Allen and Gabby. Smiles at something unseen. "Nobody plans on it. But you can't stop the inevitable." She pulls out the hunting knife. Holds it up. Studies it.

"Carla," says Allen, "put the knife down, sweetheart."

"I've been giving it some thought, honey. We should let her kill us."

Gabby turns to Allen. "Is she talking about me?"

"They say when you commit suicide," Carla says, "you go to hell. But our daughter isn't in hell. That's why we need your help."

"I'm not going to kill you or Allen."

Allen inches towards Carla. Keeps his gaze fixed on the knife. "You're upset. I understand. But this isn't going to make anything better."

"Don't you want to see our daughter again?"

"Of course I do. I miss her just as much as you do."

"Then you know what we have to do," says Carla.

Gabby says, "They're gonna come back. Trust me. I know Nadia. She wouldn't leave us."

"They're gonna die out there. Allen, let's go see our daughter." She takes a moment to study the knife. Rubs her finger along the blade.

"Carla, I love you. I love our daughter. We'll get through this together."

Carla springs to her feet. "You haven't shed a single tear since she died."

"You don't know that."

Carla takes a step towards Allen. "Say her name."

"This is crazy," says Allen.

"Say her name, Allen. Say it. Say it. Say it. Say it."

Gabby steps between them. "How about you give me the knife?"

"You trying to keep me and my husband from seeing our daughter again?"

Allen takes a step towards them. Gabby motions for him to stop. She keeps her eyes on Carla. "Allen loves your daughter as much as you do. Don't you, Allen?"

"Of course."

Carla points the knife at Gabby for emphasis. "Who do you think you are? You don't know anything about me and my husband. Imagine being married to a man with no emotions."

Allen loses it. "It's not a fucking contest, Carla!"

Gabby turns to face Allen. Exposes her back to Carla. "Allen!"

"If you won't help us, then I can't let you stop us." Carla raises the knife. Allen sees it. Gabby doesn't. But in an instant, she brings the knife down into Gabby's back. Right under her shoulder blade. She removes her hand. Leaves the knife in place.

The inside of the body has fewer pain receptors than the skin. At first, the pain is minimal—more of a sensation mixed with something warm. Gabby knows something isn't right. She turns. In a split second, she notices that Carla no longer has the knife. That's when the message reaches her head. That sensation in her back is the knife against her shoulder blade. The warmth oozing down her back is the blood that seeps between her wound and the knife blade that keeps it plugged. Blood that at this moment oozes down her back.

"What have you done?" says Allen.

Gabby crumbles to the floor and lands on her stomach. The hunting knife sticks straight in the air.

Allen takes a knee next to her. "Hold still. I'll pull it out."

Carla grabs Mr. Giggles. "I'm going to be with my daughter."

Allen watches as she sprints out the front door. He grabs the knife that's lodged in Gabby's back. She flinches.

"Get this thing out of my back," she moans.

Without a care, a countdown, or any patience, he pulls the knife out of her back.

Gabby wails from the pain.

Allen drops the knife next to her. "Keep that in case we don't come back."

Blood pours out of the wound. Shock washes over her. She can't muster the strength to argue with him. All she can do is watch as he rushes out of the cabin.

Allen stops in the front yard. Scans the area for any sign of Carla.

There is none.

Deep in the woods, the voice is faint, but it's her. "I'm here! Please! Take me to my daughter!"

Allen takes off towards her voice. The terrain is tricky. Overgrown tree roots protrude out of the ground. He gallops over them. Ducks under branches. Maneuvers around trees. And then he stops. His face drops. "Carla?"

Carla is on the ground. Surrounded by hungry men and women, all covered in blood and green vomit. Carla lets them eat her alive. She notices Allen and smiles. "I'll see her soon."

Allen hurries to her aid. He pulls one of the men off her. As he tries to pull another one off, he gets dragged to the ground by the others. They rip his shirt open. Fingernails penetrate his flesh and tear into his stomach. Organs and entrails are pulled out of the newly formed cavity. He screams as they consume him.

Chapter Ten

Gray skies act as a bridge between dusk and nightfall. The chorus of insects and crows is gone. Replaced by the sounds of hisses and the shuffle of feet.

Howell and Nadia stand with their backs to each other. Weapons raised and ready.

"I don't agree with how you and your girlfriend are living," Howell says. "And that's my right. But I figure it's your right to do it anyway."

"Not sure how you expect me to respond to that."

"Bit of advice. Ain't no worse feelin' than losin' the ones you love."

A woman in a vomit-covered bikini emerges from the brush a short distance from Nadia.

"She's all yours," says Howell.

Nadia springs into action. Bikini woman only manages one hiss before Nadia crushes her skull with the hammer. She pulls the hammer out of bikini woman's head.

Men and women of various races, ages, and sizes emerge from the brush. All of them are covered in bright green sick. All of them hiss. All of them shuffle their feet. All of them are ready to dine on Howell and Nadia.

Howell uses the butt of his gun to bash a naked guy in the head. He turns just as a woman in a cocktail dress lunges for him. He sidesteps her, and she falls to the ground. He brings the butt of his gun down to smash her face in.

Nadia extracts her hammer out of an elderly woman's face just as a man in yellow basketball shorts grabs her. She breaks free before he can bite her and cracks open the side of his face with her hammer. He falls to the ground with a hiss. Nadia wheels around, seeing Howell's attempt to hold back two women in dresses. She hustles over to help him but doesn't make it. An old man grabs her ankle from the ground. She falls. The old man hisses as he pulls her towards him. Nadia uses her free foot to kick him in the face, freeing her from his grasp. She gets to her feet and scurries away.

A man in a blue suit stands between her and Howell. She crushes his jaw with the hammer. The impact lodges the hammer in his face. Nadia struggles to pull it out.

A male nurse shuffles towards her. She sees him and releases the hammer. She scans the area for a weapon. She grabs a rock and throws it at the male nurse. It hits him in the head and stops his progress.

But only for a moment.

"Damn." Nadia searches for another weapon. Finds a stick. Nice and thick. Pointed tip. She picks it up as the male nurse closes in on her. She holds the stick in front of her as if she's about to joust. Grits her teeth. Rushes him. Full sprint. She impales him. Let's go of the stick and watches as the male nurse struggles to figure out his new appendage.

Nadia spots the man in a suit with the hammer lodged in the side of his face. He twirls. Nadia closes in on him.

She's patient. Bides her time. When the perfect moment comes, she grabs the hammer. The man in the suit doesn't know what to do. She brings her foot up to his waist. Pushes with her leg as she pulls the hammer out. It works. She falls in one direction. Half the Infected Man's face goes in the other. He falls to the ground.

Not a moment to lose. Nadia gets to her feet. She sees Howell fight off the horde with his rifle. He's outnumbered. Six to one.

Nadia races to his aid.

The vomit-covered men and women pull him down and descend upon him. They use their teeth and fingers to rip and tear his flesh.

With all the strength he can muster, he yells through gritted teeth. "Get back to your girlfriend."

Nadia freezes.

"Go!" says Howell as the horde engulfs him. He screams.

Nadia turns to head back the way they came. A surfer dude blocks her path. She steels herself. Rushes him. In one motion, she cracks his skull open with the hammer as she races by him and vanishes into the woods.

Chapter Eleven

Gabby scoots across the floor. Muscles through the pain. She's pale. Blood adheres her shirt to her back. She arrives at Junior's bag. Opens it. Goes through it. Pulls out a sweatshirt. Tosses it aside. Searches some more. Finds an industrial-sized flask. She sets the flask between her legs. This keeps it in place while she twists off the cap with her hand that's attached to the arm that's attached to the good shoulder.

Finally, the cap comes off. She raises the flask. Sniffs it. She shrugs and then takes a swig. Grimaces. Coughs. "Moonshine?"

#

The sound of hisses, moans, and heavy steps permeates the darkness. Branches snap. Bushes shake from an unseen disturbance. Nadia plods along. Her eyes dart from noise to noise.

A sound to her left.

Another sound. This one to the right.

She freezes. Grips her hammer. Waits.

A quick scan turns up nothing. Only trees and bushes and stars in the night sky. She sighs as she studies a tree. "Damn." Panic sets in. Everything blurs as she attempts to get her bearings. More hisses. More moans. More darkness. She picks a direction. Readies herself. Sprints into the darkness.

#

Drops of blood splatter against the wood floor in the doorway to the kitchen. Gabby leans against the frame. Takes a moment to catch her breath. Weary and exhausted, she hobbles to the kitchen sink. With one hand on the counter, she kneels, opens the cabinet, and rummages through it with only her right hand. Pulls out a roll of duct tape.

With every ounce of energy she can muster, she hoists herself to her feet. Holds the duct tape in her left hand. Uses her right hand to steady herself along the counter as she inches towards the kitchen shears on the far end.

She exhales upon arrival and snatches the kitchen shears. Glances back at the main room. If she leaves the kitchen, there's nothing to steady herself against. Only the open floor. It can't be over fifteen steps. Twenty max. She takes a deep breath. With the duct tape in her left hand and the kitchen shears in her right, she takes a step. It's wobbly but successful.

She takes another step.

And another.

The blood loss has taken its toll. Her skin is pale. Her eyes are cloudy. Another deep breath. She focuses on her goal. After a couple of moments, she stumbles across the room. One step after the other in as rapid a succession as she can manage.

She makes it to the door frame. Leans against it. Catches her breath.

Drops of blood splatter against the wood floor.

#

Nadia emerges from the woods and finds herself on the bank of a lake. "Shit." She surveys her surroundings. Spots a campsite. A tent. Remnants of last night's fire.

She's on high alert as she marches to the campsite. With her back to the lake, she inspects the area and finds nothing but ash, forks, spoons, an empty bowl, and crackers. But then she sees it.

A block of cheese.

She grips her hammer. Glares at the tent. The flap is partially open. She uses the hammer to peer inside. Satisfied that it's safe, she crawls in.

Out of the lake, a naked green woman surfaces. Her body bloated from water intake. Some of the green is vomit. Some of it is algae. She shuffles onto the shore.

#

The shears and duct tape are on the floor beside the sweatshirt. Gabby stands in the middle of the room and grimaces as she raises her left arm. Through gritted teeth, she takes off her shirt. The wound is awful—a mix of fresh and dried blood. Now in only her bra, she tumbles to the floor.

She holds the flask between her legs as she unscrews the cap. Downs another sip. Coughs as she wipes her mouth with her arm. Exhales. Closes her eyes. Pours some over her shoulder and onto her open wound. Yells. After the agony subsides, she lowers the flask. Grabs the shears and cuts a square out of the sweatshirt—a square big enough to cover the wound.

Next, she uses her teeth and her right hand to rip off two strips of duct tape. She places them on the square cut out. She picks up her makeshift bandage with her right hand and places it over her wound. Winces as she presses the duct tape against the inflamed area.

#

Inside the tent, Nadia searches through a pink backpack. Among the clothes, she produces a map. Grins. Sets it aside. Goes back in. Pulls out a cellphone.

A moan from outside of the tent. She pauses.

A hiss.

Nadia waits. Tenses. Sees the silhouette of the algae woman outside of the tent. Her eyes follow her as she moves around the tent until they arrive at...

The opening to the tent. The breeze off the lake pushes the open part of the flap inward. Exposes the lower leg of the algae woman. Nadia holds her breath. Sits motionless.

The hammer sits on the ground a foot away from her.

Algae woman kneels down. Peers into the tent. They lock eyes. Algae Woman hisses.

Nadia scrambles to get the hammer.

Algae woman dives into the tent. Grabs Nadia's legs. Pulls her towards her and away from the hammer.

Nadia stretches. Touches the hammer with the tips of her fingers. She can almost reach it. She uses her feet to push against algae woman. This gives her the extra inch she needs. She grabs it and rolls over. Hammer in hand. Swings for algae woman's head. Misses.

Algae woman climbs on top of Nadia. The algae vomit mixture leaves a trail of green sludge on Nadia's clothes. Nadia takes another swing. Connects with algae woman's shoulder.

Algae woman tries to bite her. Nadia uses leverage to flip them over. Now Nadia is on top. Algae Woman cranes her neck to bite Nadia. Nadia flips the hammer, and the claw is now perfectly aligned with the algae woman's right eye socket. She raises the hammer and then brings it down into the algae woman's eye socket. With all the strength she can muster, she pulls the hammer to the side. Algae woman's skull can't handle the pressure, and the side of her head bursts open. Blood and brain matter splatter the tent and Nadia.

Moments later, Nadia emerges from the tent covered in the vomit algae mixture, blood, and brain matter. Her trusty hammer, backpack, map, and phone are in her hands.

She scans the area. Satisfied that there aren't any immediate threats, she turns on the phone and sees that there's hardly any battery left.

"Great."

#

Gabby puts the final touches on a sling made from pieces of Junior's sweatshirt. She loops it over her head and slides her injured arm into it. She leans against the couch, careful not to put any pressure on her wound. She's a mess. Covered in sweat, blood, and grain alcohol, it takes all her willpower not to pass out. As her eyes close...

Her phone rings.

Eyes pop open.

It rings again.

Adrenaline rush. She sits up. Positions her body to answer the phone. Pain shoots through her arm. She realizes the phone is in her left pocket. "Of course." She brings her right arm across her body to pull the phone out of her left pocket. It works. As soon as she pulls the phone out, it stops ringing. "No, no-no-no-no."

#

Nadia screams into the phone. "No, no, no-no. Piece of shit battery!" The phone shatters as she spikes it onto the ground.

She pulls out the map. Finds the lake on it. Uses her finger to trace a path from the lake to the cabin, then the cemetery. Smirks. Traces the route once again. "Lake. Then house. Then cemetery. I can do this."

She folds up the map and sticks it into the backpack, then slings it over her shoulder. Ventures into the woods.

#

Gabby scrolls through her phone. "Come on, come on." Finally finds the last number. Dials it. Puts the phone to her ear. Listens.

"Hey! This is your girl, Beatrice. Sorry, I can't come to the phone right now. I'm too busy being awesome. You know what to do." The phone beeps. Gabby hangs up. She

sees the radio on the other side of the room. Makes her way to it. Turns it on. Fiddles with the dials. Nothing but that emergency broadcast sound. The annoying one with the steady beep. She shuts it off.

Fatigue sets in. She leans forward and braces her head on the mantel. Struggles to stay conscious. Decides this isn't how it ends. Picks her head up. Stumbles into the kitchen. The marker on the counter catches her eye. She grabs it. Across the kitchen sits the cardboard box.

Chapter Twelve

Nadia hides behind a tree. The moon supplies the only illumination. Close by, two men shuffle past her. Both of them are covered in green vomit. Their faces are covered in blood, and stuck to the blood are black feathers. Both are unaware of how close they are to her. She waits until they vanish into the darkness, then heads in the opposite direction.

It doesn't take long before the cabin comes into view. The lights are off. Silence looms in the air. She arrives at the front door and turns the doorknob. It's unlocked. She steps in. All the lights are off. Nadia closes the door. "Gabby."

No answer.

"Allen? Carla?"

Still no answer. She flips the light switch. The bulb flickers to life. Drops of blood litter the floor. Some larger than others. Some fresher than others. Her hand shakes as she steps into the kitchen.

Gabby sits at the kitchen table. Face down. Still in her bra. Back red from the blood. Bandage intact.

"Gabby!" She races to her. Shakes her. No response. On the table is a piece of cardboard. Next to it, the black marker.

Nadia picks up the cardboard. Scribbled on it in black marker, it reads 'Nadia I'm so'

Nadia's eyes fill with tears.

Gabby coughs.

Startles Nadia. She shakes Gabby again. "Gabby! Gabby! I'm here, baby!"

Gabby comes to. Groggy from fatigue and grain alcohol. "Nadia?"

"Yes. Yes. I'm here. Eyes on me."

Gabby forces a smile. "Didn't think you'd come back."

"Of course, I came back. Where's Allen and Carla?"

"They left." She points to her shoulder. "Carla. Hunting knife."

Nadia examines the bandage. It's soaked in blood. "She stabbed you?"

Gabby shakes her head.

Nadia scours the cabinets until she finds a mug. Blows the dust out of it and fills it with water from the tap, then offers it to Gabby.

"That water may not be okay," says Gabby.

"You need it."

Nadia helps Gabby drink the water. "I need to see this thing."

"I'll be fine."

Gabby grimaces as Nadia peels off the duct tape. The wound is exponentially worse. Infection can't be far off.

"We need to get you to a hospital."

"Truck? Howell?"

"Neither." Nadia pokes the area around the wound. Gabby flinches. "I need to sew this shut."

"With what?"

The medicine cabinet in the bathroom is flung open. Nadia ransacks it. Doesn't find what she's searching for. Stoops down. Rifles through the cabinet under the sink. Nothing of use there either.

The bedroom has a rustic minimalist design. Nadia explodes into the room. Checks under the bed. Nothing. Searches the closet. Nothing but flannel up on top. But down on the floor sits a sewing kit.

Gabby remains at the kitchen table. Sips her mug of water.

Nadia enters. Drops the sewing kit on the table. Preps the needle and thread.

"You know what you're doing?" asks Gabby.

"How hard can it be?" The needle and thread are ready. Nadia moves in for a closer examination.

Gabby closes her eyes. A couple of deep breaths in rapid succession. "Wait."

"Gabby—"

"I've got an idea."

In the main room, Nadia grabs the flask off the floor and returns to the kitchen. She pours the alcohol over Gabby's wound. Pours a little over the needles.

Gabby winces. "Save some."

Nadia leaves some in the flask. Sets it on the table. Picks up her instruments.

"Hold on." Gabby grabs the flask. Chugs the rest of it. Coughs. "Okay. Now go."

Nadia gets to work. She breaches the puffy skin with the needle. Gabby grits her teeth. Tenses. The needle comes out the other side as Nadia sews the wound.

"That took forever," says Gabby.

"Got lost."

"And Howell?"

"Didn't make it." The needle is re-inserted. Gabby flinches. "Sorry, sorry," says Nadia.

"It's okay. The booze is kicking in."

"Do I want to know what happened here?"

"Carla freaked out," Gabby says. "Stabbed me in the back. Literally."

"And Allen?"

"He was kind enough to pull the knife out of my back before he went after Carla and left me to die."

"You're not gonna die."

The thread leaves a trail as it goes in and out of the inflamed skin. Nadia glances at the words scribbled on the cardboard. "You wanna tell me what you were trying to write?"

"My last will and testament."

"You going to leave me all your fancy chef knives?"

"And my recipe book."

"I would sell the shit out of that," Nadia says. "In your memory, of course."

Gabby giggles and then winces from the pain.

Nadia is almost done. A few more loops, and that should do it.

Gabby says, "What do you think we should do?"

"Head back to the cemetery."

"You sure?"

"We can't stay here. You need a hospital. Besides, I found a map."

"A map?"

"It was in a tent. By a lake."

"So many questions."

"Then I had to fight off a naked lake lady. It was a whole thing."

"Is that," Gabby asks, "why you look like that and smell so bad?"

Nadia smirks. "Found a phone."

"That was you who called?"

"Didn't mean to prank you. The battery died." Nadia snips off the excess thread. Examines her work. "Not too bad. Wanna make out?"

"I probably taste like," Gabby whispers, "moonshine."

Nadia comes around. Leans in until they are nose to nose. "Moonshine I can handle." She kisses her. They give in to each other. Everything melts away, save for the bliss of kissing someone you love.

When they finally separate, Nadia smirks. "You've tasted better."

"You've smelled better."

They laugh. Nadia helps Gabby to her feet. The second Nadia lets her go, Gabby stumbles.

"Easy there, tiger."

"I might be a little... drunk."

"Never a dull moment," says Nadia.

"Grab the map. Chart a course."

The map covers the table. "I'm thinking if we head north," Nadia says, "we would run right into the cemetery."

"What if we wait until... daylight?"

"You want to stay here?"

"Per...haps."

Nadia inspects her. "Your shoulder makes me nervous. I'm not sure how long until it gets infected. If it isn't already." She turns her attention to the map. "If we head north, we should be fine. Hopefully, with it being dark, it'll be harder for those things to see us."

"Harder for us to see... them too."

"True."

"We do this"—Gabby uses the table to steady herself—"we can't, cannot go around them. That's how... we got turned around before."

"We'll fight our way through."

Nadia's confidence brings a smile to Gabby's face. "Okay. We can... we can do this."

"But first."

#

Nadia cuts another square out of Junior's sweatshirt. She tears two strips of duct tape. Next, she applies another makeshift bandage to Gabby's back. Then helps her put on a flannel from the bedroom closet. When finished, she takes a step back to admire her work.

Gabby's injured arm is back in the sling. In her other hand, she holds Junior's hunting knife.

Nadia says, "Someone told me New York has a pretty legit music scene."

"That's what they call... common knowledge."

"After we get through this, I was thinking, if New York still exists..."

Gabby's face lights up.

"If you don't mind a plus one," says Nadia.

"New York will be... good for us."

Chapter Thirteen

N adia and Gabby creep out of the cabin and across the front yard. As they reach the edge of the woods, Nadia turns to Gabby and raises a finger to her lips. Drunk Gabby responds with a thumbs-up and a wink. Into the woods they go.

They traverse the woods. Darkness surrounds them. Only a glimmer of moonlight seeps through the treetops.

Nadia hears something. Pauses. Holds Gabby's arm to get her to stop. They wait in silence. It's too dark to make anything out.

Gabby tugs on Nadia's arm and whispers, "I'm gonna need you to hold my hair."

"Be a boss bitch and choke it down," Nadia whispers back.

Footsteps. Heavy. Slow. It's impossible to tell how many pairs of feet.

Nadia determines the direction of the steps. Pulls Gabby towards a nearby tree. Settles her behind it. Then she goes to hide behind the tree next to it. Turns back to Gabby. She uses eye contact to implore her to keep quiet. And also not throw up.

A shirtless man emerges from the darkness. His bare chest smeared with green vomit and dried blood.

Gabby closes her eyes as her stomach prepares to betray her.

Nadia shifts her focus from Gabby to the shirtless man and back to Gabby.

A baseball player in full green splattered uniform steps out of the darkness and follows the shirtless man. Right behind him, a woman in a floral dress covered in green puke lurches into view.

Nadia rolls her eyes. The shirtless man is right by Gabby. If she tosses her cookies, he will hear it.

Gabby drops her knife. Puts her one usable hand over her mouth.

Nadia clocks the baseball player and the woman in the floral dress. The shirtless man passes them. He's still not far enough away to consider it a win.

Gabby closes her eyes. Gags.

The baseball player stops. As does the woman in the floral dress.

The shirtless man heard nothing. Continues on his way.

Gabby doubles over. She can't fight it any longer. She erupts. Vomit spews out of her. Luckily, it's not green. It's good old-fashioned *I-drank-too-much* vomit.

And there's a lot.

The baseball player, the shirtless man, and the woman in the floral dress all turn to Gabby.

Nadia leaps out from behind the tree. Uses the claw of the hammer to rip open the baseball player's stomach. He watches as his entrails spill onto the ground. Without hesitation, he grabs a handful and crams them into his own mouth.

Gabby continues to throw up.

Nadia makes a beeline for the woman in the floral dress and swings the hammer once she's within reach, and connects with the woman's face. The hammer gets lodged in her skull. She topples. Brings Nadia down with her.

The woman is dead, but Nadia can't get the hammer out of her face.

Gabby remains doubled over. Heaves again. The last bit of vomit sloshes out. The shirtless man shuffles straight for her.

Nadia still can't get her hammer out. "Gabby! Behind you!"

Gabby takes a deep breath. Grabs her knife. Spins. Rams the hunting knife into the bottom of the shirtless man's chin and up into his skull. He dies instantly. She pulls the knife back down. Rushes to Nadia. Arrives as Nadia extracts the hammer.

"What happened to holding it in?"

"I feel better. Not great. But better."

In the darkness, a symphony of hisses and moans and shuffling feet.

"We need to get to that cemetery."

"Gimme a sec." Gabby rushes over to the area where she threw up and takes something out of the bushes.

Returns to Nadia with the stuffed frog. Mr. Giggles. She offers it to Nadia. "In case you want to hold any concerts later."

Nadia takes it. Stares at it. "Thank you." She stuffs Mr. Giggles into her bag, and they slink off.

Nadia leads as they push aside branches as they move through the gloom. There's little to no visibility.

"Somebody help!" shouts a woman in the distance.

Nadia turns to Gabby. "Should we—"

"What about the cemetery?"

The woman cries out once again, "Please, no! Don't!"

Nadia pleads, "We can't just leave her."

"Please!" the woman begs. "I'm not one of those things!"

A volley of gunshots pierces the air.

A man laughs.

Then another.

And another.

Gabby turns to Nadia. Eyes full of fear. "There's nothing we can do for her. We need to get to that cemetery before we run into them."

They head north at a much quicker pace. Gunshots create a melody in the darkness. Hisses and maniacal laughter supply the chorus.

Gabby struggles to keep up. Slows to a stop.

Nadia notices. Goes back to her. "We have to keep moving. They're—"

"I know. I just need a moment."

More gunshots.

More laughter.

A searchlight beam pierces the darkness.

Nadia pulls Gabby down onto the ground to hide. Gabby winces from the pain in her shoulder. The light scans the area but never sees them. Unseen voices fill the night air.

"You see anything?"

"No, sir."

"Could have sworn I heard something."

Nadia and Gabby remain in the dirt. Careful not to make a sound.

"One of them infected is over there. See it?" a man says.

Gunshots.

"Over there."

More gunshots.

A female voice says, "Come and get some ole' girl!" More gunshots. Automatic weapons. Rifles. Handguns.

Nadia and Gabby keep their heads in the dirt.

The air fills with laughter and the occasional gunshot. Soon, it recedes into the darkness. Nothing left but silence.

Without a word, Gabby and Nadia agree that it's safe to get up. They pull themselves out of the dirt and haul ass. Nadia helps Gabby along. They duck branches. Stumble over tree roots. Dodge shrubs and rocks. Finally, they see it. The clearing. They will themselves forward until they burst out of the woods and into the cemetery.

But it's not dark.

They raise their hands to shield their eyes from the high beams of four different trucks. All pointed right at them.

Members of the local militia surround the vehicles. Every one of them has their guns trained on Gabby and Nadia.

Nadia steps forward. "Please. Don't shoot. We're human."

Thornton lowers his assault weapon and steps forward. A man in his 50s. Full camo and a knowing smirk. He places a knuckle over his left nostril and blows snot out of the right nostril. "Keep your weapons on them."

Gabby says, "That's unnecessary. The fact we're talking to you—"

"I'm sure you heard the President. Leader of the free world needs us folks to do our part." Thornton spits. Rubs it into the mud with his boot.

"We're not those things," Gabby protests.

"At first glance," Thornton says, "you might be right. But you could have been bitten."

"We haven't," says Nadia.

"Never can be too sure. We are at war, after all."

Mohr, a stout woman in her forties, peeks from behind her assault rifle. "Sir, maybe you can have the boys check them for bite marks. That one's in a sling."

"Not a bad idea. Ladies, we're gonna need you to strip off them clothes so me and the boys can have a better view."

Gabby says, "Not happening." She snatches Nadia's hand for emphasis.

"She was stabbed. Not bitten. I swear to you," says Nadia.

Thornton motions towards the drawn weapons. "These guns mean this isn't a negotiation."

"I agree," says Nadia. "This isn't a negotiation."

Thornton grins. "I don't need your consent. We're at war."

Gabby releases Nadia's hand and readies her knife. "We've survived much worse than you people."

"I'm gonna give you one more chance to strip out of them clothes on your own. You refuse, and the boys here will come do it for you."

Tense silence. Nadia readies her hammer.

"Suit yourselves. Let's see if these ladies got any bite marks."

The militia members lower their weapons and march toward Gabby and Nadia. Grinning and leering as they draw closer.

A young militia member named Werner eyes Nadia and Gabby. He stops. Pulls out his phone. Studies it. Glances back at Nadia and Gabby. "Ahhh, sir."

"What is it, Werner?"

Werner never takes his eyes off his phone. "Maybe we should stop for a second."

"Everybody hold on a sec," says Thornton.

Everyone stops. Gabby and Nadia exchange a quick glance, unsure if this is good news or bad.

Werner makes his way over to Thornton. "I think these girls saved my mom." He hands him the phone.

Thornton studies it. Glances at Gabby and Nadia, then back to the phone. "Yeah. That's them all right." On Werner's screen is the picture taken by the older lady they saved in front of the diner.

"Let them through." Thornton hands the phone back to Werner. The militia members turn and head back to their vehicles. "Why didn't the two of you say you were freedom fighters?" Thornton chuckles. "Could have saved us both a bunch of stress."

Gabby and Nadia remain battle ready.

Thornton motions for them to lower their weapons.

They don't.

"Where you headed?" he asks.

Nadia replies, "New York."

Thornton studies them. "Hell of a walk."

"Our car's on the other side of the cemetery," says Gabby.

"Need an escort?"

Nadia finally lowers her hammer. "We can handle ourselves."

Thornton laughs. "I'm sure you can."

Nadia and Gabby head towards their car. The ground is littered with the bodies of dead men and women covered in green vomit and blood. The militia vehicles roar to life in the background. Once at the car, Nadia sets Mr. Giggles in the backseat and fastens his seatbelt. She sets the hammer down on the seat next to him. She stares at the hammer for a second, then picks it back up and makes her way to the front of the car, and gets in behind the wheel. Gabby sits next to her. She sets the hammer in Gabby's lap. "I think this belongs to you."

Gabby picks up the hammer and examines the strands of hair that have dried in the blood. "It belongs to us."

Nadia asks, "Can you grab my phone from the glove box?"

Gabby uses her good hand to get the phone. She glances at the screen as she hands it to Nadia. "Half battery."

"Nice."

"You still want to go to New York?"

Nadia keys the ignition. "I don't care where we go."

Gabby takes a sip of the fountain drink and frowns.

Nadia notices. "Isn't that flat?"

"Yeah. It's pretty gross."

"We'll get some snacks on the way."

"Don't you want real food?"

"Snacks are real food. Plus, where are we going to get real food?"

Gabby rolls her eyes. "Valid point."

Nadia puts the car in gear, and they drive off.

THE END

SIGN UP FOR MY AUTHOR NEWSLETTER

Be the first to learn about Eric Williford's new releases and receive exclusive content!

https://thedefpix.com/

Author's Note

Once upon a time, this book was a screenplay titled *Quarancheese*. The pandemic was drawing to a close, and I, as a lover of zombies, thought there was something that could be fun about adding the undead to the covid situation. After all, what isn't enhanced by flesh-eating zombies?

Also, it's important to note: I don't dig cheese. Grilled cheese sandwiches, ugh. Mac and cheese? No, thank you. I do like pizza. I also enjoy nachos, but only if they have shredded cheese that's been melted. No pump action cheese for me. Lasagne is one of my favorite foods. But I won't touch one of those string cheese things. Nor will I eat a cheeseburger.

I have a complicated relationship with cheese.

That's how this story came to be. Mix equal parts pandemic insanity, a love of zombies, and a disdain for cheese, and... voila!

Huge thanks to the team who helped me make this thing. Thanks to Emma Jane of EJL Editing for holding my hand through things that are probably pretty obvious to more seasoned authors. Thanks to Paola Llerenas for the beta read and the encouraging feedback.

Thanks to all my family and friends who have ever checked out a screening of my films, given this a read, streamed something I made, or saw me at a party and asked, "What are you working on?"

And, of course, thanks to my wife, Allison, who is always there to offer encouragement and support. This profession is a crazy train, and having loved ones who help you keep this madness on track is important. It also helps when that person is honest with you when your ideas are less than great.

Eric Williford

August 2023

Anaheim, CA

ABOUT THE AUTHOR

Eric Williford grew up in Northern Virginia, where he spent his time playing sports and consuming late-night B movies he was too young to watch. This love of Roger Corman, Troma, and exploitation films transformed into an award-winning career as an independent filmmaker. With his debut novella, *The Dead Ate Cheese*, he looks forward to bringing his playfully grim sensibilities to lovers of dark genre fiction.

https://thedefpix.com/